JUST GO TO BED

BY
MERCER MAYER

A GOLDEN BOOK • NEW YORK

Golden Books Publishing Company, Inc., Racine, Wisconsin 53404

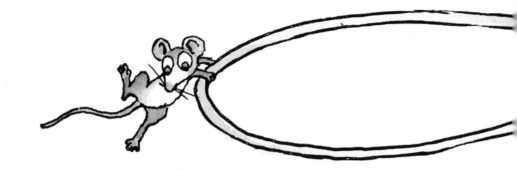

I'm a cowboy and
I round up cows.
I can lasso anything.

Dad says…

"It's time for the cowboy to come inside and get ready for bed."

I'm a general and I have to stop the enemy army with my tank.

Dad says…

"It's time for the general to take a bath."

I'm a space cadet and I zoom
to the moon.

I capture a robot
with my ray gun.

Dad says…

Dad says, "It's time for the
sea monster to have a snack."

I'm a zookeeper feeding
my hungry animals.

Dad says…

"Feeding time is over. Here are the zookeeper's pajamas."

I'm Super Critter
flying over the city.

I'm a train engineer
being chased by bandits.

Dad says,
"The bandit chief
has caught you
so put on
your pajamas."

But I'm a race car driver
and I just speed away.

Dad says, "The race is over.
Now put on these pajamas
and go to bed."

I'm a bunny hopping around my garden.

Dad says…

"But I'm a bunny and bunnies don't sleep in a bed."

Mom says, "Shhh!"
Dad says, "Go to sleep."

Well, maybe a tired bunny
could sleep in a bed...

just this once.